S0-AYO-307

DEC 15 2008

I'm Going To **READ!**™

These levels are meant only as guides;
you and your child can best choose a book that's right.

Level 1: Kindergarten–Grade 1 . . . Ages 4–6
- word bank to highlight new words
- consistent placement of text to promote readability
- easy words and phrases
- simple sentences build to make simple stories
- art and design help new readers decode text

Level 2: Grade 1 . . . Ages 6–7
- word bank to highlight new words
- rhyming texts introduced
- more difficult words, but vocabulary is still limited
- longer sentences and longer stories
- designed for easy readability

Level 3: Grade 2 . . . Ages 7–8
- richer vocabulary of up to 200 different words
- varied sentence structure
- high-interest stories with longer plots
- designed to promote independent reading

Level 4: Grades 3 and up . . . Ages 8 and up
- richer vocabulary of more than 300 different words
- short chapters, multiple stories, or poems
- more complex plots for the newly independent reader
- emphasis on reading for meaning

LEVEL 4

Library of Congress Cataloging-in-Publication Data Available

2 4 6 8 10 9 7 5 3

Published by Sterling Publishing Co., Inc.
387 Park Avenue South, New York, NY 10016
Text copyright © 2006 by Harriet Ziefert Inc.
Illustrations copyright © 2006 by R.W. Alley
Distributed in Canada by Sterling Publishing
c/o Canadian Manda Group, 165 Dufferin Street
Toronto, Ontario, Canada M6K 3H6
Distributed in Great Britain and Europe by Chris Lloyd at Orca Book
Services, Stanley House, Fleets Lane, Poole BH15 3AJ, England
Distributed in Australia by Capricorn Link (Australia) Pty. Ltd.
P.O. Box 704, Windsor, NSW 2756, Australia

I'm Going To Read is a trademark of Sterling Publishing Co., Inc.

Printed in China
All rights reserved

Sterling ISBN 13: 978-1-4027-3087-0
Sterling ISBN 10: 1-4027-3087-X

For information about custom editions, special sales, premium and
corporate purchases, please contact Sterling Special Sales
Department at 800-805-5489 or specialsales@sterlingpub.com.

BOWLFUL OF RAIN

Pictures by R.W. Alley

Sterling Publishing Co., Inc.
New York

CHAPTER ONE

It was a rainy day.

A gray day.

A not-that-much-to-do day.

Hank and Sophie were neighbors.

They were playing at Sophie's house.

Hank and Sophie played checkers.

And cards.

And jacks.

'But Sophie got restless.
"Let's get a bowlful of rain," she said.
"What a dumb idea!" said Hank.
"It's not dumb!" said Sophie.
"We can do lots of things with a
   bowlful of rain."
"Like what?" Hank asked.
"Let's get the rain," said Sophie.
"Then you'll see what we can do."

Sophie went to the kitchen and
got a big plastic bowl. Hank followed
Sophie outside. Sophie found a
good spot to put the bowl.
She said, "Let's wait on the porch
so we don't get wet."
"It's going to be a long wait!" Hank said.
"Nope. It won't," said Sophie.
"Because it's pouring!"
"How many raindrops do you think
  it will take to fill the bowl?" Hank asked.
"Lots," said Sophie. "Maybe a thousand."
Hank and Sophie watched the raindrops
plop into the bowl.
Plop! Plop!

Sophie was busy counting—393 . . .
394 . . . 395 . . . 396 . . . 397 . . .
But Hank was bored.
He said, "If the bowl doesn't fill up soon,
I'm going home!"
"Just wait!" Sophie said. "It's filling."

"The bowl's full!" yelled Hank.
"And I'm going to get it!"

Hank and Sophie
raced to the bowl.

"Let me carry it!" said Hank,
pulling the bowl away from Sophie.
Sophie yelled at him, "Hold the bowl
straight, or you'll spill the rain!"
Hank yelled back, "Don't shout! I know
exactly how to carry a bowlful of rain!"

Hank put the bowl on the kitchen table.
"Now what are we going to do with it?"
he asked.
"Well, I'm thirsty!" Sophie answered.
"So I'm going to take a drink of rain!"
Sophie took a few sips.
"Don't drink too much!" yelled Hank.
"Now what?"
"I know," said Sophie. "My hands are dirty.
I'll wash them."
Sophie stuck her fingers into the bowl.
"Don't drip too much!" yelled Hank.
"Leave some for me."
"Okay, okay, okay," said Sophie.

CHAPTER TWO

"Now what?" Hank asked again.
"I know!" said Sophie. "Let's mix colors."
    Sophie knew just where to find
    red and blue food coloring.

"I'll squeeze the red," she said.
"And I'll squeeze the blue," said Hank.
"Now we have a bowlful of purple rain!"
    they said together.

"Yup," Sophie answered. "Let's put it
in the freezer."
"But it will be a long time before anything
happens," Hank grumbled.
"Not that long," said Sophie. "We can play
while we wait. What do you want to do?"
"Go outside," Hank answered. "It's just
drizzling. Maybe we can find worms."
Hank and Sophie looked for worms.
But they weren't easy to find.

Sophie found a fat slug.

Hank found a little bug.
But no worms.

"Let's look under that rock,"
  said Hank.
"Okay," said Sophie. "I'll lift it."
"Bet you can't," said Hank.
"You're too weak!"
  Sophie lifted the rock easily.
  She really felt like dropping it on
  Hank's foot, but she didn't do it.
  She held the rock.
  And Hank looked.
"There are worms down here,"
  shouted Hank. "Two of them.
  And they're wiggling. Wiggling
  because they've got no place to hide."
"I'm getting tired of holding this rock,"
  said Sophie. "So let's switch. You hold
  the rock and I'll watch the worms."

Sophie handed
the rock to Hank.

"The worms are trying to wiggle under
the earth," said Sophie. "I don't think
they like the light."

"So I'll cover them up," said Hank.

"Careful!" said Sophie.

"Don't squash them!"

"I'm no worm squasher!" yelled Hank.

Then Hank said, "Let's go inside
and take the bowl out of the freezer."
Hank opened the freezer.
Sophie grabbed the bowl.
"We don't have purple rain anymore,"
she said. "Now we have purple ice!"
"What can we do with a bowl of purple ice?"
asked Hank.

"I know," said Sophie. "I'll put the bowl
on my itchy mosquito bite!"
Hank didn't have any mosquito bites.
But he did have a bump on his knee.
So he put the cool bowl on it.
"It feels good," he said.
"I knew it would," said Sophie.

CHAPTER THREE

"What else can we do with a bowl of ice?"
   Hank asked.
"I think we should fill the sink with water
   and put the bowl in," said Sophie.
"Will it float?" Hank asked.
"I think so," said Sophie.
   Sophie put the bowl in the water.
"It's floating!" shouted Hank.
"Now we have a floating ice boat!"
"We can name this boat PURPLE ICE,"
   said Sophie.

"Look!" said Hank. "The ice is melting.
 Our bowl of purple ice is turning into
 a bowl of water!"
"So we'll rename it," said Sophie.
"We can call it PURPLE WATER."
"I don't want to call it PURPLE WATER,"
 said Hank. "I'm tired of this game."
"But it's fun," said Sophie, "and…"

Before Sophie had a chance to finish,
Hank tipped the boat and pulled
the drain plug.
SWOOSH!
Down the drain went the purple water.
Too bad!

The empty bowl was upside down.
Sophie turned it over and half filled it
with water.

"Now what?" Hank asked.

"It stopped raining," said Sophie. "I'm going
to put this bowl of water in the sun."

"Why?" asked Hank.

"I can make things disappear, too!"
said Sophie.

Hank did not believe Sophie.

How could she make the water disappear?

"Are you coming?" Sophie asked.

"I'm coming," answered Hank.

And he followed her outside.

CHAPTER FOUR

Sophie put the bowl down.
"I don't know how long it will take,"
she said. "But the water in this bowl
is going to evaporate."
"Evaporate?" Hank said. "What's that?"
"The water is going to disappear,"
said Sophie. "It's going to turn to vapor.
It's going to vanish into thin air."
"Where did you learn that?" Hank asked.

"From a book," said Sophie.

"And do you know what else?"

"No, what?" Hank asked.

"The water's not going to disappear forever. It's going to come back as rain."

"Are you sure?" Hank asked.

"Pretty sure," said Sophie. "If you don't believe me, go to the library and check it out."

Hank looked at his watch.
It was time for him to go home.
Sophie said she'd watch the bowl
of water every day.
"And I'll put a bowl of water on
my windowsill," said Hank. "You can
check your bowl and I'll check mine."
"Okay," said Sophie. "See ya."
"See ya," said Hank.

Sophie checked the water every day.
At first it didn't look like anything
was happening.
Then slowly . . . slowly . . .
the water began to disappear.
Sophie saw a line around the inside
of the bowl where the water used to be.
"It's evaporating!" she said. "I'm going
to call Hank and tell him."
She dialed Hank's number.

"Hi," said Sophie. "The water in my bowl—
it's almost gone."
Hank had completely forgotten about
his bowl.
"Wait a minute," he said. "Don't hang up.
I'll go upstairs to check mine."
Hank ran upstairs.
He ran back downstairs.
"Sophie," he yelled, "my bowl is empty!
The water is gone. ALL GONE!"

Sophie was surprised.

Surprised that the water in Hank's bowl
disappeared before hers.

He must have had a smaller bowl,
she thought.

Or less water.

Or a sunnier place.

"Bring it over and show me," said Sophie.
"I don't believe you."

Hank ran into Sophie's yard,
holding the empty bowl high in the air.

"Look!" he yelled. "It's empty!"

"I told you the water would evaporate,"
said Sophie.

"Let's see your bowl," said Hank.

He saw the little puddle of water
still at the bottom.

"It will evaporate," said Hank, trying
to make Sophie feel better.

"I know it will," said Sophie.

"Do you want to stay and play?"
"Okay," said Hank. "Let's play jacks."
Hank and Sophie played jacks.
Then it started to rain.
"Wait!" he said. "Don't make
any moves until I come back."
"Where are you going?" Sophie asked.

"Outside," said Hank. "I'm putting
  this bowl in the rain."
"That sounds like a DUMB idea!"
  said Sophie with a grin.
"It's the BEST idea!" said Hank. "How
  many raindrops do you think
  it will take to fill the bowl?"

SCIENCE FUN

Collect your own bowlful
of rain. How long does
it take to fill up?

When blue and red are mixed together, they
make purple. What color do you get when you
mix red and yellow? Blue and yellow? You can
use paint or food coloring for this experiment.

Put a bowl of water
and an ice cube tray
in the freezer.
Which one
freezes first?

Go to the library and
ask for help finding
information about
evaporation.